SECOND EDITION
Illustrations by Dave Chisholm

ISBN 978-0-9955913-8-7

Alan Noake is a maths tutor and IT consultant who lives in the sticks near Sandwich in Kent. He is married. No kids. Alan has been a scout leader for over twenty-five years. He loves travelling and his big crazy dream is to visit Antarctica.

'Clerb' is his very first attempt at publishing.

Hopefully it is not his last!

for Sonia -

the best sister on
'Gravel'!

CLERB

An alien time travel adventure story*

(*involving yoghurt!)

by Alan S. Noake

FOREWORD (or should that be 'BACKWORDS'?)

Rooting about in the loft of a house that you have lived in for ages can be a dangerous activity. Especially if there are no loft boards! But recently I stumbled across a paper file in a pile of my sister's old belongings that we have had stored up there for years for her. In it I discovered (what I believe to be the only surviving printed copy of 'Clerb') a short book I wrote some twenty-seven years ago now. I created the character of Clerb especially for my sister one summer just to while away the hours while I was supposed to be doing some 'very exciting' computer programming work. Anyhow, I dusted off the pages, set about scanning them in one by one and here is the final finished result... exactly as it was written back then. Well almost exactly – to be honest I have corrected a few spellings and typographical errors – but the story stands unadulterated. (A really good choice of word as I have not tried to 'Adult' up the story choices made by my younger self.) So now that self-publishing is just a little bit easier than way back then when I first wrote it and sent it off to a traditional publisher only to be disappointed I thought it might be fun to finally share it with the world. Clearly, I was influenced by two huge gods of funtastical literature - Douglas Adams and Terry Pratchett – and I would never claim to be in the same league but since some of the jokes created by my younger self still made me chuckle nearly three decades later it would be a shame not to spread the love and the laughter. Enjoy!

Alan S. Noake

*Sandwich, Kent, 25th March 2017 on a cold Saturday afternoon, About Tea Time**

**Okay, okay – so just a little bit of Monty Python influence too – but I did write it all on my ownsome, honestly.*

CLERB 1

Clerbs grow on trees. That is if the tree happens to be in the right mood. You don't just get your average tree sprouting out in hundreds of Clerbs - just like that. It takes years of dedicated practice. And of course, it takes a good deal of boredom. A tree must be bored. One might think that being a tree would always be boring, which is true. Ask one. But I am talking about an intense special kind of boredom which surpasses anything we humans are used to. And it doesn't just happen to any tree. And it doesn't just happen. Many factors must be present. Many factors must be able to be present. And many factors must send their apologies if they are unable to be present. For instance, take rain. If it was raining, then a tree would find it very difficult to be bored. Can you imagine trying to be bored with all that water dripping all over your branches? Well I know you haven't got branches - but you get the general idea. Suffice it to say things must be just wrong. And then a tree might suddenly be extremely bored. And then a Clerb might grow on it - if it wants to. So, you see why you don't see many Clerbs doing their shopping in Sainsbury's on a Saturday morning. They are hard to come by. Even harder if you shop on a Tuesday.

However, after saying all that, which I wish I hadn't, Clerbs do exist. I haven't seen one, but I do think I believe that they might try to exist a little bit - for the sake of my sanity, and above all for the sake of this story...

Clerb lived just outside London, in a flat in Wensleydale, on the far side of a Scottish loch, overlooking the French Riviera. He lived alone. No one knew he was there. And no one would have been bothered if they did know he was there. But he was. And he hated it that way. It was an ordinary flat. Seven rooms built simultaneously in the same airspace - summed up as a bed, a cooker, a basin, a table, a couch, a doormat and a jacuzzi full of erotic, sorry exotic, bathing salts.

One particular night, connected with no day in particular Clerb awoke with a jolt. He could find no logical reason for being awake so he went back to sleep. The next morning, he awoke without a jolt to find the sun flickering all over his bed-covers. Four hours later he got up - and then went back to bed again with a black speckled slice of toast and a large mug containing a suspicious kind of lukewarm liquid. One more hour later he finally ate the toast. And half an hour after that he got out of bed again.

Three things would instantly strike you if you saw Clerb. Firstly, his hair. Secondly, his arm. And thirdly, my fist, because you'd have seen him and I haven't.
He has long hair right up to his forehead and one particularly large arm protruding from his stomach. Apart from that, and the fact that his pyjamas are indigo, he is a pretty normal Clerb - short, stocky and bouncy with a big frown constantly on his face.

Anyway, on this particular morning, now nearly afternoon, after the particular night connected to no yesterday in particular, Clerb proceeded to get dressed and after wiping his feet on the doormat left the flat. He turned left and made his way along the High Street carefully so as not to be seen by you or me, or just by you with my fist hitting you, or just by me, or by anyone. He yawned, he looked around, he opened his eyes, yawned and then looked around again. He made his way past the pram wheels of prams containing busy babies with their mums pushing them anywhere they didn't want to go. He dodged

briefcases carried by businessmen packed full of rubbish, the businessmen that is. And finally, after being bruised and even more bruised by an assortment of very-hard-low-down-things he reached his destination. Sainsbury's. (Well what did you expect in a High Street - Buckingham Palace?)
You may not or may be wondering how a Clerb with an extremely indiscrete arm extending from his belly could enter a very well-known High Street store without causing a commotion? I could ask you the same question. In fact, I just did. What I mean is you could ask me the same question. Anyhow he did. And no one noticed. Perhaps because they didn't care, perhaps because Star Wars was on at the Empire the previous night, but mainly because they didn't notice.

Clerb was intending it to be an ordinary shopping trip, at an ordinary High Street store, on a very ordinary Saturday morning. So, he was quite surprised when it was. He chose his groceries, he even bought a 'Ballpoint Pen Repair Kit' which was hung up next to the canned soup, and what's more he even payed for it all. Not that the cashier would have blinked an eyelash, as the big hand threw the money at her, while she was plucking them. But Clerb was semi-honest and anyway he liked it when she nearly accidentally plucked half an ear off. Not that he smiled about it. Not that he ever smiled about anything.

That was Clerb's problem. Well not Clerb's problem as such. But it would be a problem in our opinion even though Clerb didn't consider it a problem. In fact, the real problem is that we think Clerb has a problem related to him not smiling. He doesn't. He wouldn't smile even if he did have a problem with not smiling.

The main thing to be understood is that we must understand whether we in our heart-of-hearts want Clerb to smile once in a while for our own sake or whether we just want him to smile once in a while because he hasn't got a problem realising that he hasn't got a problem with not smiling. I myself think he has a problem. You may be of the opinion that it is me that has the problem. That's your problem. Back in Sainsbury's things were finally starting to go terribly wrong. Which should make this story slightly more interesting. At least more interesting than just finishing it when Clerb takes his shopping home, for instance. However, some of you may be of the opinion that that would be a fabulous and very agreeable idea. So just for the rest of us to get our own back the story is going to get more interesting. That is to say it is going to go on longer. And, why shouldn't it? Life is unpredictable. So there.

"I can't quite fathom it out" said Bert.

"You can't quite fathom it out" said Ernest.

Bert Trenchbottom sank into despair. Some weird space creature with a very embarrassing arm was ruining his peaceful Saturday morning shift, and he had to contend with Ernest. Ernest Wriggle tried desperately to be intelligent. He tried to be Bert's friend. He even tried skiing once, but that's another story. The point is he tried. And this annoyed Bert intensely. Which in turn encouraged Ernest to try harder. He leaned over the switches, and buttons, and levers, and other various things to pull, press and generally control things with that were scattered over the security console.

"What?" he whispered.

"What what?" replied Bert, by now bubbling with anger at his partner's lack of security skills.

"What can't you fathom out?" Ernest asked in some new speech form lower than a whisper. Bert gave up. There and then. He had never really wanted to be a security guard. He had never really wanted to be an anything. There were so many things that he hadn't wanted to be, that he was spoilt for choice when he realised he had to be one of them. Such is life. No offence towards security guards. It is just Bert didn't like the job anyway and working with Ernest hardly improved matters. He decided to spell out the situation in plain English to save further confusion. He looked Ernest directly in the eyes and explained carefully. "There on the screen," he pointed up to the security monitor which showed a view of the cashier now filing her nails and of an empty walkway and conveyer belt, "I saw something a moment ago."

He gathered his thoughts before he continued. This next bit was going to be difficult. He turned back to Ernest who was now sitting forward in his seat with an irritating expectant look on his face. "I saw a...," he cleared his throat "Martian," he finished.

Ernest managed to change the irritating expectant look into an even more irritating disappointed look. He didn't say anything for nearly 30 seconds. He hated being made fun of and what was ten times worse was been made fun of by Bert. He felt that Bert would go kilometres out of his way to make fun of him.

"Of course, you did," he said.

It was a classic 'Cry Wolf' situation. No wolf had ever cried louder. Bert sank further into despair than ever before. He realised that he had pulled at least two of Ernest's legs off with previous jokes - and that made him feel rotten. It also left Bert without a leg to stand on. He just sat and sulked. Clerb, on the other foot, not having another hand, was unaware he had been spotted for the first time ever - at a chance of one in two.

Obviously, his luck was down today. But as he was not aware of this he frowned and walked out of Sainsbury's closely missing a very large pram and three briefcases.

CLERB 2

I honestly don't know what is going to happen next. Neither do you. Unless you have already read this book before. In which case, you have more idea about what is going to happen next than I do. If so could you write and tell me so that we can get the story well and truly written...

Right, thanks to a very confused reader from East Grinstead who reminded me how the story continues I can now continue telling it. I think.

Four hundred metres down the same High Street three women were discussing the problems of nappy rash. Exactly three hundred thousand light years to their immediate left a now very confused reader from East Grinstead was flittering through time itself. And five weeks and three hours north of him was a planet. The planet was called by four names - the most popular of which was HOME.

Its inhabitants preferred HOME to Qwistlethorpia, Efoplasmitar or the very tedious accurate name of Univ1Gal4Sect2Plan18 for the obvious reason that HOME begins with an 'H'.

The Homians, as they shall be called for more simplicity, are very old. In fact, each is so old that the chance of a particular Homian dying in your lifetime, or mine for that matter, is at least seventeen-to-one against. That is why Spearshake, the great Homian playwright, didn't write many tragedies - the death scenes could get slightly tedious. Rather than snuffing it politely, the dying tend to make more of a HOME run.

"How come all the inhabitants are old?" - I hear you say. Go on say it. (Not out loud, or people will look at you, and then they might not buy this book!!! Cover up the cover if they are staring at it. Thank you.) The simple answer is that it is a kind of 'Old People's Planet'. Years ago, when the surrounding planets decided that someone living on them was getting a bit too senile to cope with they had shipped them off to HOME. End of story. Or was it?

Well not quite, because these Homians, ran into a stroke of luck - in the form of the river Qwistle. Not an ordinary river by any standards.

It all happened very early on in the planet's history when Uggerly Sappleworth, the first of the interstellar O.A.P.s (Over Active Pensioners), was taking a riverside stroll. The Qwistle was about so wide and so deep. (Imagine me showing you with my hands.) And it stretched so far. It had a bank on both sides of it to stop the liquid overflowing. The liquid itself was as totally unlike water as you can get without it not being a liquid. It was black. It was sludgy. And it was very un-wet? Uggerly was ambling along minding his own business. You could argue that because he was walking along a river bank that he wasn't minding his own business. His own business was a local hearing-aid manufacturer. So, it could be said that that business was not being minded. But no-one would hear it being said anyway - due to a local lack of hearing-aids. Anyway, let it be said, even if no-one hears, that Uggerly was ambling along minding those parts of his business not attached to hearing-aids. Apart from his left ear perhaps. Early complications in the Sappleworth family had left old Uggerly with the scars of rejection, and he was bitter. The whole family had voted unanimously that he should be sent to HOME.

And that had been on his 70th birthday. What a birthday present - an extra-long holiday to nowhere of your choice! He found it difficult to forgive them and hoped many of them would end up somewhere worse. If there was any place worse?

This particular riverside walk was one of Uggerly's escape-from-it-all walks. He usually contemplated dying, and reincarnation and bridge evenings, and the like. This was perhaps his intention on this walk, but for one reason, or the same reason again, he didn't get that far. No sooner had he got to the small path on the river bank and had ambled a few metres along it when something very accidental occurred. He assessed the situation. He tried the calm approach. It didn't work too well. So, he panicked. Being smothered head first in a thick, dark and almost dry liquid might have had a similar effect on most of us I guess. Uggerly went one better. He really panicked. And then he drifted into oblivion... which took a good deal of drifting.

Uggerly awoke, a lot longer than three minutes forty-four seconds later, to find himself sprawled on the Qwistle's opposite bank, he felt very alive, and very dry, and thought it was all over. He could not have been more wrong. For days afterwards other

Homians marvelled at the improvement in the availability of hearing-aids and most of all in Uggerly's new lease of life. Many of them stumbled, limped and even crawled down to Sappleworth Ears Inc. to see him bounding around and generally being the original Over Active Pensioner. They were fascinated and very intent on finding out old Sappleworth's secret. He would probably have been immediately obliging if he himself had realised his secret.

It finally came to him. "Of course," he said to himself. "How could I have been so stupid?" But these things often do take time to become apparent - you know, like 'Eureka' and all that bath business. By that very afternoon the entire population of HOME were in the Qwistle and wallowing around in it - totally by accident - of course. It seems that the Qwistle has some sort of energising quality - and as theory states - a planet full of thousand-year olds can't all be wrong. Unless it is something in their breakfast cereal, perhaps?

So, the Homians are very old. They are also extremely tall, stupid and exceptionally good at accounts, but those are other stories. They also know about Clerb, which as you might quite rightly have guessed, is our story...

CLERB 3

Meanwhile, five weeks, three hours South, three thousand light years to the right and now a bit more than four hundred metres down the High Street Clerb was still dodging killer-shoppers! He frowned at them, unseen and annoyed. He hated Saturdays. His favourite day was Wednesday. But personally, I think Tuesday has something to offer. Tuesday. The day that had to come into this story somewhere, because the plot goes on longer than a week. Tuesday. The day I love dearly. Tuesday. The epitome of all that is just, and fair, and good. The mere sound of the word is music to my ears. The mention of this day awakens hidden things which are asleep somewhere. Pick whichever day you want. But Tuesday is mine. It doesn't begin the week. It doesn't end the week. It is not even nearly the end of the week. It is not the middle of the week. And it is definitely not at the weekend. It is just Tuesday.

Clerb, as I said, liked the middle of the week. So, Saturdays were right out! All the bustle and hustle was not up his street. (It was up the High Street.) He preferred quiet places like parks and meadows and padded cells. Shopping always gave him a nasty headache and headaches always gave him a craving for Paracetamol and a lack of Paracetamol was always one good reason for going shopping. He unlocked the flat door with his shopping piled up to his chin. He opened the flat door. He went through the flat door. And he shut the now very flat door. However, he was moderately surprised to find himself standing in his flat. Previous experience had taught him to expect the worst. On two occasions, he had found himself in the middle of a lake, and once he had walked into a BBC studio in the middle of Blue Peter. So, he liked to be prepared. This time it was his flat. He hastily made his way to the table as the piled-up shopping began to give way in its precariously balanced state. He made it just in time. He only had to stop a rather excited can of soup from rolling off the edge. He had just begun to sort his shopping out when the doorbell rang. Clerb considered the situation. He pondered over it. He thought about it. He even speculated about it for a moment. Finally, he decided the best way to find out why his doorbell was ringing, for the first time ever, was to open the door.

"You look like the sort of person who needs some warmth in their life," said a rather tall salesman without even looking at Clerb. "Can I interest you in the new range of super extra-thermo, hyper-deluxe, ultra-heating radiators for you and your family to keep up with the Jones' and be one step ahead of the rest?".

Clerb thought that the salesman looked very old. He gaped at him in wonder. Clerb wasn't used to visitors. Clerb was used to being ignored. He just stood there and frowned as usual. The tall, old salesman continued, "They come in all different shapes, colours, sizes and have a number of different settings for all seasons and can be installed at your request within twenty-four hours and are guaranteed for three years and run at a very reasonable cost and..." It was all too much for Clerb. He was lost in a maze of radiators. His vivid imagination was having serious problems managing to imagine itself, let alone all the possible permutations of radiator design that were whirling through it. He fainted.

The tall, old salesman continued. It took him a good few more minutes of contented continuing before he realised Clerb had feinted. He put down his suitcase.

He then knelt down beside Clerb who was starting to come around.

"Quick Clerb shut the door - so we can talk," the salesman whispered. He hadn't realised his act would have such a considerable effect on the little fellow.

"Okay," said Clerb and shut the door. "But..." he said feeling very dizzy and confused. "...who are you? Where are you from? How do you know my name? What do you want from me? Why do you look so old? And how much is a red, slim-line, deluxe radiator with a heat modifier?"

The old man looked down at Clerb. Clerb frowned up at the old man. "My name is Bewtiffle Sappleworth and I am a salesman, but I don't sell radiators, I sell hearing-aids for my father's company. I am from HOME."

"Aren't we all," remarked Clerb.

"No, I mean the planet HOME. You may know it as Univ1Gal4Sect2Plan18."

"Oh, that planet - of course." Clerb was not taking things seriously. A typical Saturday.

"All the Homians know your name Clerb. We need your help. We are all very old. And the red ones retail at about 185 pounds."

Bewtiffle went on to tell in glorious detail how his father had been the first to have primitive swimming lessons on HOME. And then droned on about all the other things we already know about and don't ever want to hear about again. Clerb sat there patiently and politely - and got earache.

"But how did you know about me?" Clerb finally asked. This is the interesting bit for us. But it is a bit far-fetched. It is only a story though! Here goes...

Bewtiffle told him.

"I don't believe you," said Clerb.

"It's true," said Bewtiffle. "No one on Earth can see you unless you are holding a tin of canned soup, or a can of tinned soup for that matter. Some hippy student actually lived in this flat and we displaced him from this dimension so that you could live here. You are a Clerb."

"I know I am Clerb! This is stupid."

"No, I said you are a Clerb! They grow on trees. And fall off like leaves. But I suppose you don't remember that bit?"

"Yes, I do! It was extremely painful. But are you suggesting that you made that happen?"

"The odds are logically against it happening - we just did something odd to the odds which turned out to be very odd indeed."

"Are you calling me odd?" Clerb demanded. The dizziness had left him. He was determined to understand all of this.

Bewtiffle went on to explain lots more odd things to Clerb. But we can find them out as we go along, because they are not very interesting out of their natural setting. A bit like fish out of water. They tend to have a lot of trouble breathing and look very different. So, we'll have a good look at them in a fish tank. Also, my inverted comma key on my typewriter is asking for a day off. So, we shall end this chapter, alright?

Finally, Clerb and Bewtiffle left by the now completely flat door.

CLERB 4

Ernest Wriggle dropped the binoculars. He had had enough of Bert's games and wanted to go home. Bert Trenchbottom picked up the binoculars and watched as the salesman left the flat opposite.

"Perhaps the little fellow is going to a fancy-dress party," suggested Ernest.

"A fancy-dress party is one thing, but Sainsbury's is another!" said Bert. "Come on," he said and rushed towards the door.

"Where are, we going?" Ernest cried as he followed Bert through the open doorway.

"To talk to the salesman."

"But we don't need any radiators."

Bert left the conversation behind him and dashed across the road. He caught up with the salesman. Ernest was only moments behind. Bert tapped the salesman on the shoulder and when the old man turned around he couldn't believe his eyes. He was older than old. He was an antique antique.

"Can I help you?" said Bewtiffle beautifully. Clerb was standing right next to him enjoying the feeling of being invisible. He was pulling faces at Ernest. "Stop it!" exclaimed Bewtiffle, not so beautifully.
"Pardon?" asked Bert.

"I said can I help you?" Bewtiffle tried to ignore Clerb's latest facial masterpiece.

"Umm, we are from Sainsbury's. We are looking for a Martian with one arm. We have reason to believe you have just sold him a radiator."

Bewtiffle wasn't quite sure where the planet Sainsbury's was. But he was sure that he wasn't going to stick around to find out. He opened the door to his radiator salesman's sales van and after letting Clerb clamber across the driver's seat he got in. The long pause holding the van door open looked quite odd to Bert and Ernest.

"I am sorry I can't help you gentlemen," shouted Bewtiffle as he started the engine. "Perhaps, you have had a few too many late nights. Martians indeed." He chuckled and sped off. Bert and Ernest stood speechless and stunned and confused and lost. They looked at each other. Then they looked at the now very distant van. Then they turned and walked slowly back to their stakeout. Both now determined to get to the bottom of this. They took it in hour-long shifts. In this way, they managed to watch Clerb's flat constantly for an hour and a half. It was Ernest who gave up. He stormed out of the stakeout and walked determinedly across the road. He rang the doorbell to Clerb's flat. A hippy came to the door. "Peace man," the hippy said. "I just had a really freaky spaced-out trip."

Ernest was beginning to think that someone had it in for him. That morning he had set off for a quiet day as a Sainsbury's' security guard. Now he was questioning a hippy about the whereabouts of an extra-terrestrial creature carrying tinned soup.

The hippy was loving it. His life had never been better.

"With only one arm you say?" he asked the four Ernests in front of him with a mellow voice. Then he giggled. Ernest saw it was useless. He gave up and made his way back to the stakeout to wake his partner. The hippy slid down the doorway and watched the eight of them go. It had been a long day.

CLERB 5

I could tell you what happens to Clerb and Bewtiffle next. I could even tell you what happens to Bert and Ernest next. But all that can happen in some other chapter. This is what was happening to Uggerly - it is slightly more urgent and is definitely more interesting.

There was no place like it. HOME was a very weird planet. If we go out into space a little we can get a better view. That's better...you can just make out the vountains and mallies. The whole planet is swirling in a thin green wispy cloud. A bit like pea soup, but more cloud-like. And all over the surface the glistening river Qwistle can be seen meandering along like a drunken snake.

If we zoom in a bit closer, we can have a good nose at Oldar. It is the capital city of this small planet. It boasts three bingo halls, four post offices, a number of bridge clubs, and Sappleworth Ears Inc. - the biggest HOME grown business ever.

Closer still, and we find the aged figure of Uggerly Sappleworth addressing the people of Oldar who are all crowding outside his factory. They have all come to find out about the threat to their planet's existence - which was a pretty good reason for coming.

"My son should have been back on HOME yesterday," voiced Uggerly stepping forward. "I have sent him for our Clerb. It is time to make use of it. We created it for helping us in situations such as this. They don't grow on. . .I mean they... umm... they don't exist too often. So, when they do they must be made use of."

The crowd was obediently silent. They listened carefully to the master-swimmer's words of wisdom. Uggerly wondered how to explain the next bit. Threats to a planet's existence were not the easiest things to explain to anybody. He tried.

"Now don't panic," he began. He was physically shaking and had a comforting look of extreme terror on his face. "What I am about to say will doubtless make you want to dash home and hide in that little dark cupboard under the stairs. But don't panic. Listen carefully. And don't panic. Panicking will get us nowhere. So, don't do it. We must go about this in an orderly and calm fashion. I don't want to see even a tiny bit of panic. Do I panic, I mean, do I make myself quite clear?"

The crowd nodded as one, like mechanical donkeys above a mine.

Uggerly panicked!

The crowd panicked!!

Far above the green mist a lack of light moved across the sky darkly. There was a noise which was deafening. There was a louder noise which wasn't heard because the first noise was deafening - but it was obviously louder because the distant vountains could be seen to shake. Then there was a long dark silence in which nothing was seen or heard. Then the lights came on.

Uggerly and a couple of thousand other Homians just gaped in amazement as the music began to play. It was loud and very irritating. The planet was dazzled by an enormously big "Space Coach". That was the only way of describing it because that was what was written on its side in gigantic neon letters "Interstellar Galactic Tours – Space Coach." It was literally an enormous double-decker coach filled with hundreds of tourists. All of the tourists were wearing bright coloured T-shirts with things like "Surf City" and "Sun Fun", and clicking away with flashing cameras, and saying "Gee Whiz", "Spiffing!!" and "Cor, mum look at those old fogies."

A loud Tannoy system began to speak, like they do. It said "The planet HOME. Identifiable by its eerie green fog. Population eleven thousand. An incredible average age of 670. It is an old people's retirement paradise. If you look closely you may see some of the friendly old folk..."

If Uggerly was a picture of friendliness, then pigs really do eat 3 Shredded Wheat. To say he was not happy would be on the ground floor of a block of under-statements. He was livid. He was mad. He was angry with a capital 'A' - that is - he was Angry. He felt humiliated and he could see that the crowd felt the same way. Most of them had already set off for the little dark cupboards under their stairs. The few that were left were seriously deciding to invest in stair cupboards.

The Space Coach glowered down at the Homians with bright coloured window-eyes and a gold stripe mouth. The tourists pressed against the eyes like specks of provocative dust and jostled for a good view of the little planet.

"Please return to your seats ladies and gentlemen," droned the Tannoy system. "Our next stop is the constellations of Exio Major. Feel free to give the old folk a happy wave of thanks."

Then the immense Space Coach moved away dispersing green mist behind it and let in the daylight chunk by chunk. HOME was back to semi-normal. Uggerly felt drained. He slumped to the floor. He wept. A number of younger old Homians came over to comfort him and wept too. It was a sad day. There was lots of weeping, crying, and even a good deal of wailing.

"Where's that son of mine with our Clerb?" Uggerly asked himself. "Perhaps something can be done. Otherwise we are helpless." Then he thought about his son Bewtiffle. "We are helpless," he said. An hour later the next Space Coach came by.

CLERB 6

Can you hear it? The loud hiss of steam. The swearing. And the sound of someone kicking something metal. You guessed it! An over-heated radiator on a radiator salesman's sales van. What an advert! What a mess! Bewtiffle was desperately trying to sort it all out. He was the one who was swearing. He was guilty of doing the metal-kicking as well.

Clerb was sat on the kerb. He was content to be going nowhere. He didn't want to go off heroically and save worlds from existence threats. He frowned and watched as Bewtiffle hopped up and down clutching his foot and yelling. Clerb's external expressions were all wrong. They were all opposite to how he actually felt. That is why he laughed and smiled when he was upset, which never seemed to happen. And why he frowned when he was happy - or when he found something funny - which was generally all the time. It was confusing, but could prove useful - as in this particular case. If Bewtiffle had thought for one minute that Clerb thought the situation was at all funny, he would have put a very permanent expression onto the little fellow's face.

Bewtiffle finally decided, when his foot was beginning to go numb, that he and the van needed to cool down. He sat down next to Clerb. His legs were so long his knees hovered next to his ears. He tried to calm down. They sat there in silence. They didn't say anything. Clerb didn't say anything. Then Bewtiffle suddenly didn't say anything either. After Clerb hadn't said anything for the third time Bewtiffle stood up and walked back over to the van. He sat in the driver's seat. He put two hands together and looked at the sky with his eyes closed. He turned the ignition. The van said something - in a sort of primitive coughing language.

Five minutes later Clerb and Bewtiffle were on their way again. Bewtiffle drove with pride and had a determined look on his face. Clerb, on the other foot, sat in petrified despair admiring as much scenery as he could in the vain hope that he may eventually become a stationary part of it again.

"How are we going to get to HOME?" asked Clerb, instantly regretting starting a conversation.

"Have to get to a yoghurt factory before nightfall," answered Bewtiffle in a very matter-of-fact manner.

"Of course, how silly of me... I should have guessed." Clerb was now prepared to believe he really did grow on trees and that it hadn't all been a bad dream. If these Homians had wanted help wasn't there an easier way than subjecting him to yoghurt factories. It was more than he could cope with. Anyway, it couldn't get worse?

CLERB 7

There is no point in trying to explain why Bert was annoyed. I think the name Ernest Wriggle explains everything. Bert was not happy about Ernest making decisions of his own. If he had wanted to make decisions of his own, then he should have consulted his partner first. Or at least someone of sound mind. People couldn't start making personal decisions on their own - it just wasn't acceptable.

"What do you mean there is a hippy living there?" demanded Bert. "We both saw the Martian go in. Does this hippy know he's living with a Martian?"

"That's just it," answered Ernest. "The hippy doesn't know anything about the whole affair. He was totally spaced-out while it was all happening."

Well that was that. Bert and Ernest had no lead. They didn't even have a dog. All they had was a jumbled tale of radiators and hippies. I think you'd agree that probably wouldn't stand up in court. Not even if they got a nice judge who liked to give the benefit of the doubt.

So, that really was that. Whatever that was? That couldn't be this. That would mean this could be that. And that might make this sentence stupid.

Bert and Ernest decided to pretend none of it had ever happened and privately they were both unsure that it had. They left the stakeout and set off back to Sainsbury's, and normality? They were both very quiet and kept their thoughts to themselves. But seen as this is only a story we can find out what they are thinking... nosey aren't we?

Ernest was trying to do his best to make an effort to seriously stop thinking about the Martian. He tried to think instead about his wife and his two small children. His wife's name was not normally said in public due to the obvious lack of compassion it showed her parents must have had - it was Missledroppy. Her friends, and Ernest, called her

Miz. Ernest and Miz had met on an escalator. They had bumped into each other head on. No prizes for guessing that it was Ernest who was going down the up-escalator. Miz had kindly offered to help him extract his shoelace from the moving steps. A man like Ernest needed a woman like Miz behind him. He did tend to leave a trail of chaos and devastation wherever he went.

The two small children consisted of various screams and noises cunningly disguised as cute little girls. Their names were Elly and Jess. Ernest would have preferred something more appropriate like Brat and Horror to warn innocent people, but Miz had insisted that he would regret calling them that in later life. He didn't regret it at all.

Bert was definitely trying not to forget about the Martian. He was not married and didn't have any kids that he knew about. He was convinced that seeing that small, hairy little fellow with that very prominent arm, singular, was really the start of a breakdown. Had he been working too hard lately? Perhaps he should try one of those other jobs he didn't want to do. Perhaps he should go on holiday and lose some luggage and spend hours in places he didn't want to be in. It just didn't make sense. If he had imagined it all then how come Ernest had seen the Martian go into the flat as well, carrying a can of soup, or was it a tin? Surely two people couldn't imagine exactly the same thing could they?

"Does anything strike you as odd about that old salesman's behaviour Ernie?" asked Bert.

Ernest snapped out of his thoughts and considered the question. He looked at Bert with an 'I thought we weren't going to talk about it look'. Then he realised Bert had noticed it as well.

"You thought that pause when he got in the van was weird as well didn't you?" said Ernest rhetorically.

They both looked at each other like Holmes and Watson back on the case. They now had a lead. It was about time they found a dog.

"What was the name of the radiator company? It was written on the side of the van - Shuthouse, Shothouse, Shi. . ."

"Hothouse," said Ernest before Bert could have any more guesses.

"Hothouse, that's it, and I was going to say Shi..."

"Well we won't go into what you were going to say. Let's find this Hothouse before things cool down and get this business over with. My Miz will be waiting up for me. Worse still she might have cooked me a meal as well."

They reached the entrance of Sainsbury's and casually decided not to bother going in to explain. Instead they set off to find Hothouse Radiators. It had to be more interesting than explaining why they wanted to spend the last hour of their shift chasing a Martian. Shift work never had agreed with either of them. It was one of the many parts of the job that made being a security guard even less appealing than it already was."

Bert found the company name in a Yellow Pages that conveniently had most of the 'H' entries left in it. Ernest stood outside the phone box and did his best to hail a taxi. Why when you needed one did they stop their usual trick of mowing down innocent bystanders? Anyway, one finally came along and it was 'For Hire'. Ernest flagged it down with a sort of Worzel Gummidge impression in the middle of the street. Crows would have been proud to be scared by him. Bert rushed out of the phone box clutching a yellow piece of paper which looked suspiciously yellow. The two of them jumped into the taxi as it sped off taking most them with it.

The man from Hothouse must have been on one of those 'Customer Bad Relations Courses'. He was small with a beard. His middle name just had to be 'Awkward'.

"Look here gentlemen, I have better things to do than find out if one of my salesmen is over 600 years old," he said. He was grumpy, obviously depressed, sad-faced, miserable, bitter, angry, and irate. Not the ideal soul for getting information out of.

"Surely," attempted Ernest. "...surely, you would have noticed if someone who works for you is slightly older than the norm?"

"Why?" asked the man obstinately.

"Why, because it's a pretty obvious thing to notice!" butted in Bert, backing his friend up.

Ernest had gone up a millimetre in his estimations.

"I don't think it is."

"Well of course you don't think it is otherwise you would have noticed it, wouldn't you?"

The man hadn't thought of that.

CLERB 8 - INTERMISSION

If you would like to make your way to the end of this chapter by reading it in a refreshing way then you can take advantage of some of the fabulous words and sentences written to take your mind off the story for a while.

There are a wide range of nouns and verbs joined together for your delectation. If you are thirsty there are some adjectives like WATERY, FRESHLY and THIRST-QUENCHING-LY. If you are hungry there are some tasty similes like... He was as fat as a big, jam doughnut with cream and sugar and a lovely crisp golden texture and a soft fluffy light bit inside.

For those among you who are very keen on popping to the loo during intermissions there are available some long drawn out descriptions of waterfalls, rivers, streams, lakes, ponds and other pleasant gushings of running water from various sources.

Anyone left who is not queuing up for some ice-cold dramatic irony or a meaty metaphor in a bap - can stay here with me and discuss the story so far... good isn't it?

CLERB 9

Three questions spring to mind.

One: Where were we?

Well Clerb was being taken to a yoghurt factory by Bewtiffle. Bert and Ernest were desperately trying to interview the Hothouse manager with no luck so far. And Uggerly is presently making plans to open a stair cupboard business.

Two: What happens next?

Clerb and Bewtiffle arrive at the yoghurt factory. Bert and Ernest actually find out from the Hothouse manager that there had been one old fool who had hired a sales van for a very persuasive sum of money. And Uggerly will be talked about in a minute - don't be so impatient!

Three: What is the ending?

Now come on now, that would spoil reading the rest of the book for you. If you are that interested, then write to me and I will tell you how it ends.

Right, shall we continue? (Ooops, make that four questions.)

Uggerly will be discussed in about 45 seconds.

Until then I would like to take this opportunity to introduce a new character into the story. Don't worry about Uggerly I will mention him briefly in 30 seconds time. But this new character is much more integral to the plot. I wouldn't want to let you read on without you knowing a bit more about this new character. Otherwise there could be real complications. So, it is very, very crucial that you know what he is like. His name is...

Uggerly felt like he was intruding on the story, but the 30 seconds were up and he had to come back into it somewhere. He was still impatiently waiting for his son and the Clerb. Every hour the Space Coach was driving him to INSANITY! Not literally of course, although I have heard it is quite a nice seaside resort.

The Space Coach arrived every hour, on the hour without fail. It was the same each time. The Tannoy delivered it's irritating, dreary speech and then the coach moved on dispersing the green clouds so much so that they hardly had time to look eerie, green and cloud-like again before the next coach came by. It had been like that for three days now and Uggerly was near the end of his tether.

At present Uggerly is talking with the elders of Oldar. These were the older elders of Oldar as opposed to the not-quite-so-old elders of Oldar or the Oldar younger elders who weren't yet of age to be invited to meetings of this ilk. Uggerly spoke. The others listened. This was easier than Uggerly speaking at the same time as the others or no-one speaking and everybody listening. It was the best method of getting things sorted out.

"Elders of Oldar I have gathered you here today to talk about Plan C. As you know Plan A involves Bewtiffle and the Clerb. And Plan B doesn't exist because we haven't got a 'B' in our alphaset which is reliable enough to work broperly. It does have a havit of bbbbeing inconsistent. So, it is for this reason that we must resort to Plan C."

"Get on with it Uggerly," bellowed Nighsley who was the head foreman at Sappleworth Ears Inc. He was not happy about the product expansion into stair cupboards. He thought they would make very uncomfortable earrings.

"Yes, come on Uggerly," stressed Whickid. His name reflected his pleasant, easy-going manner. He was impatient to hear Plan C. He raised his eyebrows sternly and beamed at Uggerly like an owl about to attack a mouse.

Uggerly took the hint. "Plan C is of course only a last resort plan," he continued. "It is in reserve to Plan A and Plan B. We will officially cancel Plan C if Bewtiffle and the Clerb arrive or if all the typewriters and voice boxes on Home suddenly decide to bet all their 'B's right. Is that understood by everyone?"

"Yes," said EVERYONE scratching his forehead.

Uggerly then listed the main elements of the plan. (Hydrogen, Helium, Lithium, ...sorry I couldn't resist that!) "We will form two groups which we shall call the reds and... umm... the slightly-off-reds for clarity. The reds shall comprise of myself, Whickid, Horryblee, Eval, Rhottan and Terryblee plus the smaller half of the younger elders. That leaves Nighsley to lead the slightly-off-reds who will be Kighnd, Konsidrat, Frendlee, Gorjus and Super-cringy-creep-creep. They will take the larger half of the younger elders."

Uggerly stood up and eyed each of the older elders of Oldar individually. Could he really win against the enemy with this band of Over Active Pensioners? At least most of their hearts were in the right place. They would fight with their experience of life. And boy did they have a lot of that. It would be brains against brawn. It would be the battle of the age-groups. The war of the revolting O.A.P.s. They were revolting, not revolting if you see what I mean. Still it was their only back-up plan. So, having no choice he continued. "The slightly-off-reds will create a diversion to distract the Space Coach driver and tourists on the midday flight. The time now is six-thirty A.M. That gives you five and a half hours to think of something extremely distracting. Us reds are going to actually board the Space Coach somehow and go back to wherever Galactic Tours comes from. And we'll show them a piece of our minds."

"How are we going to get up high enough to board the Coach?" asked Rhottan. He was a big chap. He was presently flexing his muscles.

"Just leave that bit to me," reassured Uggerly not knowing for one minute how they were going to get up that high.

If you want my opinion. Which you probably don't. But even if you don't want my opinion - it does seem stupid for you not to read it now you have read the beginning of this paragraph. I don't know what your opinion is of Plan C, and I am quite happy for you not to write and explain your opinion to me in extremely tedious detail. In fact I don't want to know your opinion which suggests to me that you probably don't want to know my opinion of Plan C by a process of logical role reversals. So, I won't give my opinion. Apologies to those who read to the end of the paragraph expecting to hear it.

CLERB 10

At one time or another human beings have a habit of questioning their own personal existence. At other times, they decide that their existence is not worth questioning. And at very different other times some decide to not even decide whether to question anything or not. This was one of those times for Bert. He was prepared to believe anything and question nothing.

Bert was sitting in the back of the taxi again. Ernest was sitting next to him. Both of them were suffering from some kind of extreme G-force. The taxi driver was suffering from a sadistic grin.

The taxi sped on.

"How are we going to find this Hothouse van then?" contorted Ernest.

"With this," said Bert, stretching his face into even worse shapes than Ernest.

The taxi sped on.

Bert held up the AUTOMATIC EXTRA SENSORY

SUPER TRIDATIC VERY CLEVER VAN-FINDER which the Hothouse manager had handed to him as they were leaving the factory, just by chance.

"How do you use it?"

"Well you press this button marked 'WHERE IS THE VAN?' and it tells you where the van is."

"Thank heavens for modern technological advancement," said Ernest. "Well go on press the button then!"

Bert held the gadget firmly on his lap. He carefully pressed the button marked 'WHERE IS THE VAN?'.

"The van is parked outside the TAY STEE YOGHURT FACTORY," said the AUTOMATIC EXTRA SENSORY

SUPER TRIDATIC SMART ALEC VAN-FINDER.

The taxi stopped. Bert and Ernest picked themselves up off the floor. The taxi driver wound down the glass partition between the front and rear seats and spoke clearly.

"We are going completely the wrong way for the TAY STEE YOGHURT FACTORY," he said, raising his long eyebrows as if they were windscreen wipers.

Bert stared at the taxi driver.

"How did you hear that we wanted to go there when the partition was up a moment ago?" he demanded.

The partition was now up again.

"Pardon?" said the driver. Even though Bert and Ernest couldn't hear him they could lip-read the word. The sadistic grin didn't have to be heard.

The taxi did a 1-point turn. Bert and Ernest were thrown into a friendly heap at the extreme right-hand end of the back seat.

The taxi sped on.

This would now be a very good time to tell you about the character from the previous chapter who never actually got mentioned because of Uggerly's very rude interruption. Uggerly has apologised to me since then and would like it to be made public (not too public though) that he will buy us all a drink if we meet him in the pub next Friday.

Anyway, back to this elusive character who I shall now tell you about. I don't want to get side-tracked again, because I realise how annoying it can be to a reader if the person writing the story stumbles off the beaten track. And I should know. I have got the beaten-track-stumbling bruises to prove it.

So, I am not going to let it happen again. Some writers have a habit of straying so far from the point that they actually find themselves not making the point at all. Where was I? Oh yes...

The taxi pulled up outside the TAY STEE YOGHURT

FACTORY.

The partition was wound down before you could say "Jer...."

"That will be 13 pence...," began the taxi driver.

"That's cheap," said Ernest, reaching into his pocket.

"...for the entertainment and 48 quid for the journey!" finished the driver, with a massive sadistic smile. He prided himself in his sadistic smiles. He practiced for hours in front of his bathroom mirror to get them just right. And then he spent a few more hours getting them perfect.

"Pay the man Ernest," ordered Bert.

Ernest took this ideal opportunity to have another go at exerting himself. He was not going to be pushed around by Bert any longer.

"No, you pay him - I always end up paying," he said solidly. He even said the hyphen with conviction.

Bert couldn't believe his ears. That is, he couldn't believe the information going into them. He did actually believe he had some ears.

"Half each," he compromised.

Ernest agreed to this and paid over the larger half.

The taxi sped off.

Bert and Ernest turned to face the TAY STEE YOGHURT FACTORY. It was no different in appearance to any other yoghurt factory. Come to think of it - it was no different in appearance to any other factory. The only obvious difference was that the perimeter fence had a massive van-shaped hole in it. The two men made use of the rather unusual entrance.

Little things began to happen.

Ernest looked back at the fence and saw that the hole wasn't there anymore. The fence had somehow mysteriously healed itself.

Bert, on the other hand saw himself slipping through a side door into the main factory building.

Then when he and Ernest reached the door he looked back and saw Ernest and himself coming towards the door. It was all very weird. Inside the building it got weirder.

CLERB 11

Sometime after the second pair of Bert and Ernests had entered by the small side door a sales van containing Bewtiffle and Clerb smashed through the fence leaving a big van-shaped hole in the mesh.

The van screeched to a skid, slid for a while and then at a very high pitch screeched to a halt.

"The TAY STEE YOGHURT FACTORY," read Clerb out loud. "How corny." He frowned. He thought Bewtiffle had been joking.

Bewtiffle looked at the little fellow frowning at him. He wondered if they really could save HOME in time. Then he smiled because that was exactly how he intended them to save it - in time.

They left the van and walked over to the main entrance of the factory building. Bewtiffle waved his hand over the security lock 14 times whilst humming to himself. Eventually he decided to give telekinesis a miss and picked the lock in 10 seconds with a hairpin.

"Why yoghurt?" asked Clerb, knowing he would regret asking. But he just had to know. He had had trouble coping so far but yoghurt was the limit.

"Time travel," answered Bewtiffle, as if it was the answer to all of life's problems. The truth is it probably causes most of them. Clerb frowned.

"Perhaps I am ignorant, but I don't quite see the connection between the two?" said Clerb. He scratched his forehead with his hand and put on one of his extra-special frowns. A frown was the only safe way of not confusing anyone with his usually inaccurate expressions.

"What, the connection between time and travel? I assure you there is one."

"No, I was thinking more between time travel and yoghurt." replied Clerb. "Anyway, do go on."

Bewtiffle went on...

...And on...

"...so, you see by combining those particular flavours of yoghurt in just the right industrial quantities with the exact number of pieces of fruit to indicate the year, time of day and place..."

...And he went on...

"...So, you see this vat contains all that we need to save HOME."

Clerb leaned over the big vat.

"Smells good," he said, licking his lips. "How much of it do we have to eat?"

Bert and Ernest had listened to Bewtiffle's speech totally amazed. At least now their doubles had caught up with them. They had merged into them which had felt very weird at the time. But now they both felt many times the men they had felt before.

They watched as Bewtiffle stood on the edge of the vat, held his nose and then jumped in. They watched as Clerb reluctantly climbed onto the edge of the vat, hit himself on the nose and fell in.

They watched as neither came back up to the surface.

Then big things began to happen.

Crates of yoghurt began to burst all around the factory. The vat began to bubble. The doors all slammed shut. Individual yoghurt pots exploded. Especially the banana ones. Generally, there was an overwhelming presence of yoghurt.

Bert ran back to the door and found it was very shut. He grabbed Ernest and dragged him towards the big, bubbling vat of mixed yoghurt. They squelched through a sea of kiwi fruit and peach yoghurt, but eventually they managed to get to the edge of the vat.

"It's our only chance to get to the bottom of this!" shouted Bert.

"But I'm allergic to raspberries!!" screamed Ernest, as they plunged into the thick, creamy mass.

The vat swallowed them and belched.

TIME got annoyed.

CLERB 12

HOME. 11.45am. Chaos. In fact, lots of chaos. So much chaos you could fill a galaxy with it. Well at least a medium-sized galaxy anyway.

Uggerly wasn't ready.

The reds were rushing all over Oldar. They were looking for ladders, old bits of scaffold, boxes, pegs, poles and anything else for creating height. They were piling their findings up and up, but it just wasn't high enough.

The slightly-off-reds were rushing all over Oldar. They were looking for guitars, pianos, fiddles, costumes, make-up and anything else for creating entertainment. They were setting a stage show up, but it just wasn't entertaining enough.

The reds and slightly-off-reds kept getting in each other's way. This started arguments. These arguments in turn started fights. As I said it was chaos.

Still to give the Homians credit at least they were trying. Every one of them fighting for their planet. Even if it was against each other.

Imagine if you can the situation at two minutes to midday...

Konsiderat is playing a trumpet very badly.

Twenty of the stronger, younger elders of Oldar are forming a forming a human pyramid on top of the pile of ladders and junk.

Nighsley is conducting a band made up of slightly-off-reds.

Whickid, along with Terryblee and Horryblee, is helping the very irate figure of Uggerly Sappleworth to the top of the human pyramid.

And Super-cringy-creep-creep is tap dancing centre stage in a pink dress.

Chaos.

On the stroke of midday, although I don't quite know who was doing the stroking where and to whom, the Space Coach burst through the green clouds. The driver was instantly distracted by the sight of a small frog leaping from a lily pad on a pond just outside of town. He totally missed the sight of Nighsley and the slightly-off-reds playing 'Here we go round the mulberry bush...' with various instruments and dancing round the stage in various bright coloured costumes. Anyway, he was distracted.

Uggerly only just reached the top of the human pyramid in time. He couldn't believe his luck. Plan C was going to be successful. He was right next to the cargo door of the Space Coach. He grabbed the handle which swung down, thus opening the door. He swung up into the cargo bay landed on a solid floor and collapsed. Then he was falling, falling, falling...

The Space Coach had completely disappeared. The human pyramid had completely disappeared.

In fact, the only thing which hadn't disappeared was the ground which by a strange coincidence was the one thing that just happened to be coming towards him rather rapidly...

CLERB 13

TIME was troubled.

Clerb thought he was drowning. What a thought! Fancy drowning in yoghurt of all things. He splashed about with his arm which made him spin around in circles. He opened his eyes. Stupid idea.

He shut them again. How did he expect to see through yoghurt anyway? The long deep breath he had taken prior to falling in the vat was running out. He prepared himself for the worst. He would never be able to look at a yoghurt again. He would never be able to do anything again. This was the end!

It was the end of a leg. Clerb gripped tight and wouldn't let go. It was Bewtiffle's leg and what's more it had the rest of Bewtiffle attached to it.

Clerb fainted. It was becoming something of a habit to faint every time he met Bewtiffle.

However, Bewtiffle had felt the hand on his ankle and reached down and got hold of Clerb. The yoghurt was changing. It was getting thinner, more like milk. And somewhere far off Bewtiffle could hear a voice. A soft caring voice muttering...

"Are you sure we put enough hazelnuts in? I'm worried about the carbohydrate-protein ratio." said TIME, a little worried.

Then the voice faded. The yoghurt vanished. The vat, factory and world vanished. Everything that hadn't vanished so far vanished. All that was left was an air-filled void with Clerb and Bewtiffle and Bert and Ernest in it.

"Where are we?" asked Clerb, coming around.

Then he saw Bert and Ernest. The funny thing was Bert and Ernest could see him. No tinned soup either.

"How on HOME did you get here?" asked Bewtiffle, ignoring Clerb's question and staring at Bert and Ernest.

"We, uh, ...," said Ernest uselessly.

"We followed you here," said Bert helpfully.

"Wherever here is."

"Well you can damn well go back again this instant!" shouted Clerb, confused and upset.

"I'm afraid," said Bewtiffle. "That it is not that simple." He walked over to Bert and Ernest. It was quite weird walking on nothing, but he was used to it. "We are at present not anywhere so you can't go back."

It is impossible to go back to somewhere from nowhere. You can only go forwards. So, it looks like we are stuck with you!"

At that moment, the air-filled nothingness began to change into an air-filled somethingness.

Bewtiffle raised his hand to indicate that silence was in order. He stood still and waited. Clerb, Bert and Ernest also stood still and waited for whatever it was Bewtiffle was waiting for. The overall effect was quite stunning to look at. (I'm afraid you'll have to wait for 'Clerb the Movie' to get the most out of this bit. Just take my word for it - it looked stunning.)

A haze was rising up all around our four friends. Through it they could just make out some shops and streets. Slowly, very slowly the haze lifted. They began to realise that something was very odd about the street they were in. It was bright green and very soft underfoot. Clerb thought that there was a very 'alive' feeling about it. He looked at the shops. They too were various shades of green. In fact, everything was green - the glass windows, the doors, the brickwork - everything.

Even the little sign on one door with the opening times on it was a pale green. And it all felt very 'alive'.

"I don't much like this place at all," stated Ernest honestly.

"Would you have preferred blue, perhaps?" asked Bewtiffle.

"Oh, it's not the colour I don't like - it's the people!"

"What people?" queried Clerb.

"Exactly," said Ernest. "There aren't any."

"Who says there have to be people?" demanded Bert philosophically. Suddenly, another haze rose up around them again. Bewtiffle heard the same soft caring muttering again...

"Yup," it said. "definitely the wrong amount of hazelnuts. Perhaps a few more strawberries as well. That should do the..."

Once again, the haze lifted. This time with a bit more confidence. Our four friends appeared in the middle of the same street. But this time it was full of people and there was a distinct lack of green.

"That's better this TIME," said Bewtiffle. "Now dad said we were to find a company called Galactic Tours." As Bewtiffle said this he became very aware that he was being watched by a number of nosey shoppers as well as by the three others. "Let's get out of here!" he shouted.

Clerb watched Bewtiffle push his way out of the gathering crowd. Then he watched Bert and Ernest follow after him. Clerb wondered how he could possibly save HOME by running down a street. Clerb suddenly felt very alone and scared.

The crowd had closed up and were moving in closer and closer. They were laughing at this poor little fury creature with one arm. Clerb, however didn't think it was funny. He smiled. Clerb smiling was a very rare occurrence as I have said.

Luckily for Clerb Ernest realised what was happening and reached back through the crowd. He grabbed Clerb just at the last minute. Just at the last second would be a more accurate description. Who knows what might have happened if Clerb had started laughing?

Ernest and Clerb caught up with Bewtiffle and Bert.

"What happened?" asked Bert panting.

"No time for conversations," yelled Bewtiffle. He set off again at a tremendous rate. "Come on!"

The other three followed him. The crowd, having realised that the rugby scrum was over, set off after the rugby ball. Clerb decided that he would rather be anything other than a rugby ball at that present moment, except perhaps a one-armed hairy thing created to save worlds from existence threats.

"How can Bewtiffle possibly have a dad?" shouted Ernest to Bert as they were running. "He'd be far too old."

"I don't know," answered Bert. "But I wouldn't like to meet his grandfather."

"All the Homians are very old," added Clerb knowingly. He was trying to be friends with Ernest. After all Ernest had saved him from death by rugby.

All four of them ducked behind an alley and waited for the crowd to go by. It worked. About the only plan of Bewtiffle's ever that had worked first time, but it worked.

After consulting three street maps and after using a certain amount of guess work Bewtiffle, Clerb, Bert and Ernest found the Galactic Tours building.

Clerb looked up at the gleaming new building and nearly strained his poor little neck trying to see the top. It was a big building. It was obviously a big company.

"I hope TIME is right," said Bewtiffle entering via the revolving doors.

"It's ten-thirty," said Bert looking at his wrist watch. "But I don't quite know where it is ten-thirty."

They all span into the foyer. They all felt dizzy.

"What a silly door," whinged Clerb climbing up off the carpet.

"Can I assist you in any way, gentlemen?" said a smart, elegant doorman beaming at them.

"Yes, you can," said Bewtiffle.

There was a long pause.

"If you would be so good as to tell me what it is I can be of assistance with sir," said the doorman patiently. He was still beaming brightly and annoyingly.

"You can take that stupid smile off your face for a start," ordered Bewtiffle. "Then you can show my friends and I to the meeting. That is if we are not too late?"

"Right away, sir, if you would like to follow me?" replied the doorman, beaming more intensely than before. He led the way up a long flight of steps. Bert happened to notice that the doorman was counting to himself. He just had to ask.

"Why are you counting the steps?"

"To be sure how many there are," answered the doorman.

"How many are there?" asked Bert.

"I don't know yet," said the doorman. "Someone always interrupts me when I am trying to count them."

"Sorry," said Bert feeling stupid.

Eventually they all reached the top of the large unknown number of steps. Clerb's little legs were tired. He was also panting the loudest. The doorman led them along a long corridor. At the end of the corridor was a door. The door was shut and on it was pinned a white notice with black writing...

FINAL APPROVAL MEETING FOR SPACE COACH ONE - PUBLIC WELCOME TO COMMENT

They went in. The meeting was already underway. However, the room was full of rows of connected empty seats. At the far end of the room was a long table filled with committee members who were quietly going through the motions of the meeting even though no one else had turned up. That is until Clerb, Bewtiffle, Ernest and Bert turned up.

The committee gasped one big gasp.

Our four friends sat down in the back row of seats. Everyone on the committee was struck dumb for a while.

"Don't mind us," said Bewtiffle. "Carry on."

The chairman stood up. He was a kind looking young man wearing a pink suit which contrasted pleasantly with everything else around him.

"Umm, urr," he said. His secretary wrote it down. (Only she spelt 'Urr' wrongly.)

". . .Urr, Item number six. Does the meeting think that the space coach should go past the planet HOME?"

"Don't you think it is a bit unfair intruding on the O.A.P.'s privacy," said Clerb politely. "They love and respect HOME as if it was their..., well, home."

"Yes, I suppose you are right young... what's your name?"

"Clerb, Mr Chairman, sir."

"Clerb, now there's a funny name. Yes, you have a valid point there, well spoken." The chairman turned to his pretty secretary. "Jo, would you take young Clerb's point into consideration please immediately and arrange a last-minute alteration to Space Coach One's route. What was the name of that reserve planet - Gravel or something?"

Bewtiffle smiled at Clerb.

Clerb frowned at Bewtiffle.

"Earth, sir," said the secretary.

Bert and Ernest were not smiling or frowning. They had some serious talking to do with the chairman. It took them a bad three hours to get him to change his mind a second time. Still what's three hours between planet-savers?

The chairman agreed in the end that Earth would be slightly costly to bring into the route because of it being light-years away from the rest of the route.

He eventually agreed to including a small moon called Hotams. Hotams didn't really belong to anybody, but it did have some nice geographical features which might be interesting to school parties.

Bewtiffle decided it was time to get going. All they needed now was some form of transport for himself and Clerb, and a yoghurt factory for Bert and Ernest to get back to 'Gravel' before any of this had ever happened.

The YUM EE YOGHURT FACTORY was easily found.

They all said their goodbyes before Bert and Ernest jumped into the big yoghurt vat.

"At least I won't have to explain all this to my Miz," said Ernest.

"Why's that?" asked Clerb.

"Because I am going to make Bert tell her," Ernest said with conviction.

Bert smiled, Ernest had come a long way in no TIME. Maybe he wasn't so bad after all.

"I hope this yoghurt mix is right?" asked Bert.

"Only TIME can tell," said Bewtiffle.

"Bye, then," yelped Ernest falling in next to Bert and splashing his friend with yoghurt.

TIME passed.

CLERB 14

TIME had a headache!!!

...falling, falling, falling. . .

Uggerly found himself in front of a crowd of Homians. He was terrified. One minute he had been falling towards his impending death. The next he was making a speech with a very strong feeling of **veji du**. What was it called? **Voodoo Ju**, **Duja View**, **Deva Ju** or something like that. He couldn't remember. But he could remember living this moment before - and that was all that mattered.

The crowd of Homians were staring at him.

"My son should have been back on HOME yesterday," voiced Uggerly stepping forward. The feeling of **Doodah Voo** was getting worse. "I have sent him for our Clerb. It is time to make use of it. We created it for helping us in situations such as this. They don't grow on... I mean they... umm... they don't exist too often. So, when they do they must be made use of." Uggerly wondered why the **vu dojah** was so strong a feeling.

The crowd was obediently silent they listened carefully to the master-swimmer's words of wisdom, not feeling any sense of **dover blue** at all.
Uggerly wondered how to explain the next bit. Threats to a planet's existence were not the easiest things to explain to anybody. He tried. Help me shake this **daisy goo** off he thought to himself.

"Now don't panic," he began. He was physically shaking and had a comforting look of extreme terror on his face. "What I am about to say will doubtless **deja you** want to dash home and hide in that little dark cupboard under the stairs. But don't panic. Listen carefully. And don't panic. Panicking will get us nowhere. So, don't do it. We must go about this in an orderly and calm fashion. I don't want to see even a tiny bit of panic. Do I panic, I mean, do I make myself **quite vu**?"

The crowd nodded as one, like mechanical donkeys above a mine. Again.

Uggerly panicked again!

The crowd panicked again!!

Far above the green mist nothing happened. Then there was a friendly little chugging noise. Then slowly edging through the mist came a small space scooter. And on the back of it was Bewtiffle and a small hairy fellow who was crying with joy. It was heading for HOME.

"**Deja vu!**" exclaimed Uggerly.

The crowd was confused.

TIME had a paracetamol and went to have a lie down.

The space scooter landed near Uggerly. Bewtiffle fell off and went over to his father. Uggerly embraced him and then turned to Clerb.

"I think we owe you an apology," said Uggerly and shook Clerb by the hand.

The crowd was really confused but decided that cheering seemed appropriate. So, they cheered.

Clerb looked at Bewtiffle and shook his hand. A big tear appeared in the little hairy fellow's eye. Then the strangest thing happened. He began to fade away. Very slowly. First his head. Then his body. Then his legs. Until only a short and very singular arm was left. The hand waved and then Clerb was gone.

Bewtiffle was shocked. The crowd was very confused. Uggerly stood in silence. He bowed his head. And then he whispered these words. The silence was so great that everyone in Oldar heard them...

"He has served his purpose and he has gone."

CLERB 15

I never did introduce that character to you earlier.

High up on the edge of the Oldar malley under a big spreading oak tree the unintroduced character sits writing.

He looks down at the crowd gathered around Bewtiffle and Uggerly.

He puts down his pen and paper.

He stares blankly, in private thought, at the sky.

"It's unlikely that there will ever be another Clerb," he whispers sadly to himself.

"How extremely boring," said the tree.

Printed in Great Britain
by Amazon

53586048R00050